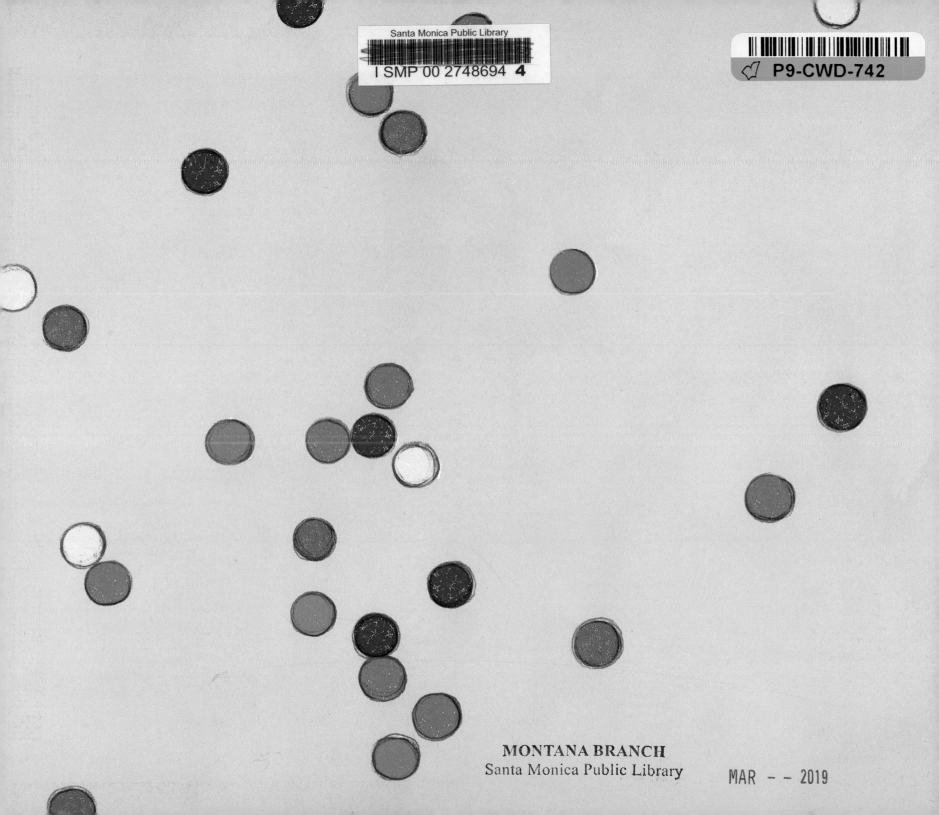

For Max Maher.
I hope you have many happy birthdays.
—J. G.

For Eleanor Muir, with love
—D. B.

# baby day

Words *by* Jane Godwin & Davina Bell

Pictures *by* Freya Blackwood

atheneum

Atheneum Books for Young Readers
*New York  London  Toronto  Sydney  New Delhi*

Today is baby's birthday.

There's going to be a party.
Happy baby!

Here come baby's friends.

Hello!

Shy baby.

Friendly baby.

Sunny baby.
Hat on, baby!

Strong baby.

Smiley baby.

Lazy baby.
Wake up, baby!

Bossy baby.

Neat baby.

Busy baby.
Watch out, baby!

Brave baby.

Twin babies.

Fussy baby.
Come on, baby,
just try it!

Waiting baby.

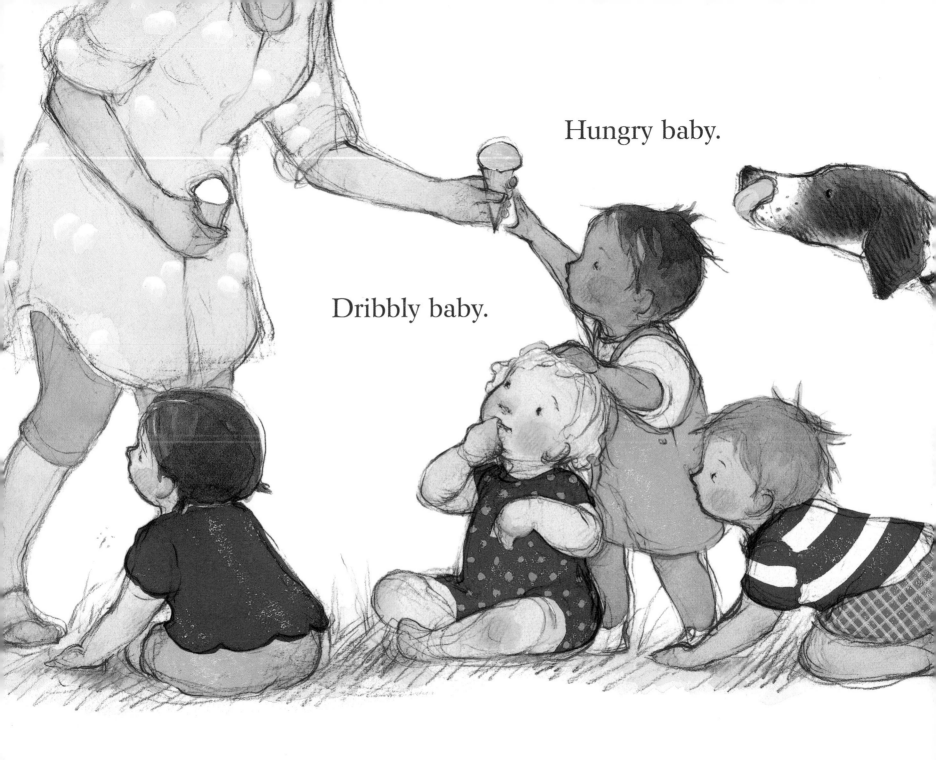

Hungry baby.

Dribbly baby.

Oh no . . .

poor baby!

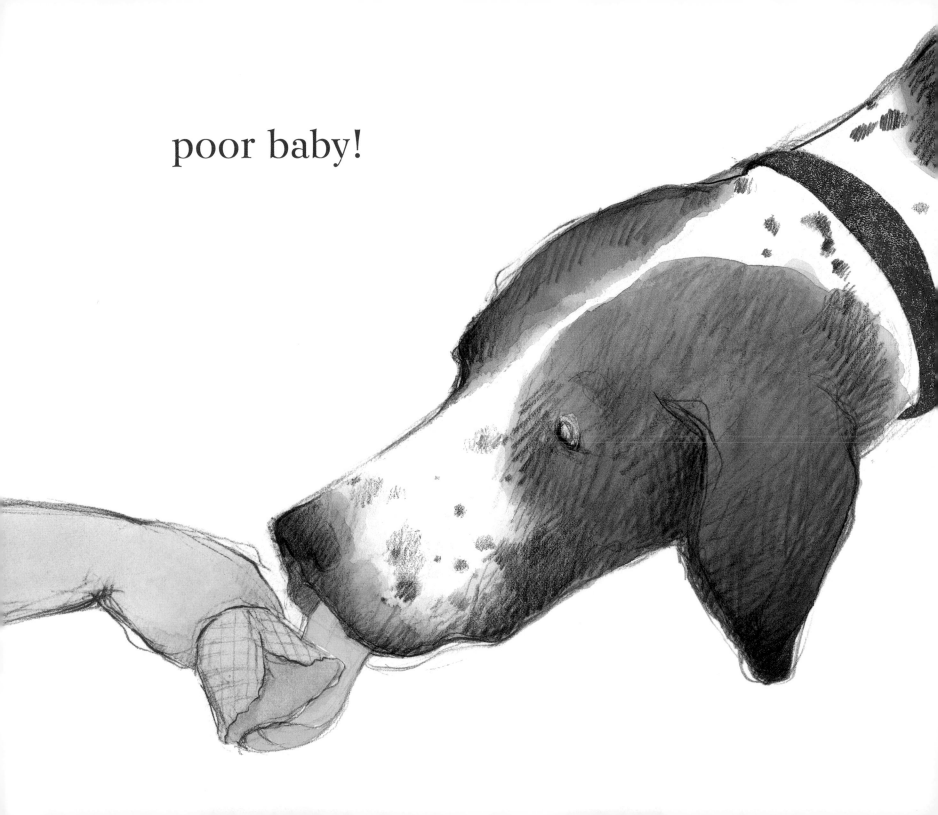

Sad baby.

Kind baby.

Loud baby.

Worried baby.

Dancing baby.
Nice moves, baby!

Come on, babies,
time for cake!

One . . . two . . . three . . . blow.

# Happy birthday, baby!

Now, smile for the photo.

Cheese!

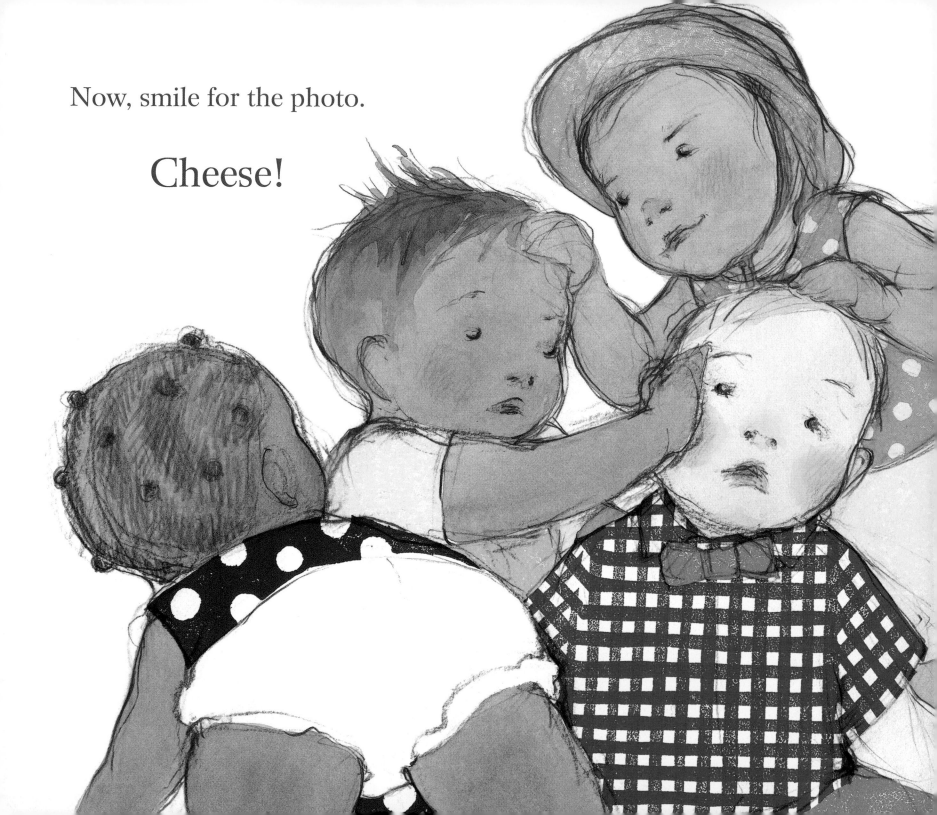

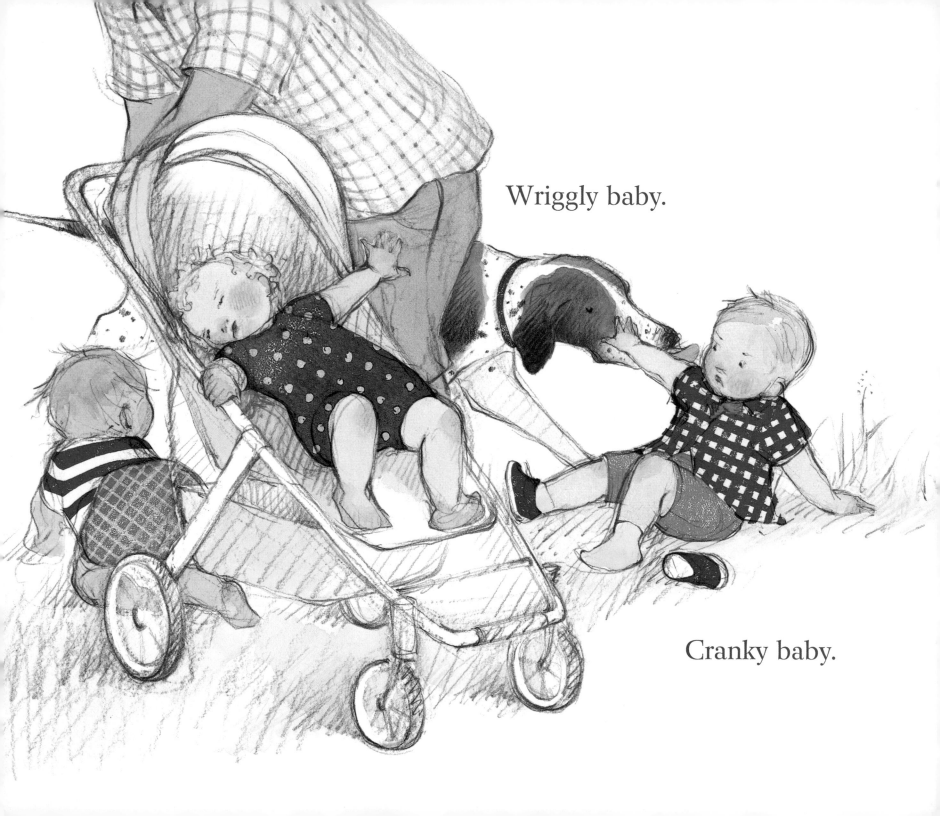

Wriggly baby.

Cranky baby.

Tired baby.

Angry baby.

Time to go home, baby.
Blow a kiss . . .

Wave bye-bye.

Bath time baby.

Cozy baby.

Bedtime for the birthday baby.

Sweet dreams, baby.

*Shhh . . .*

𝒜
atheneum

ATHENEUM BOOKS FOR YOUNG READERS
An imprint of Simon & Schuster Children's Publishing Division
1230 Avenue of the Americas, New York, New York 10020
Text copyright © 2018 by Jane Godwin and Davina Bell
Illustrations copyright © 2018 by Freya Blackwood
Originally published in Australia in 2018 by Allen & Unwin
For information about special discounts for bulk purchases, please contact Simon & Schuster Special Sales
at 1-866-506-1949 or business@simonandschuster.com.
The Simon & Schuster Speakers Bureau can bring authors to your live event. For more information or to book an event,
contact the Simon & Schuster Speakers Bureau at 1-866-248-3049 or visit our website at www.simonspeakers.com.
Book design by Lauren Rille
The text for this book was set in Wilke.
The illustrations in this book were rendered in line work and watercolor on paper,
with digitally composited oil paint lino-block prints.
Manufactured in China
1218 SCP
First Atheneum Books for Young Readers edition March 2019
2  4  6  8  10  9  7  5  3  1
Library of Congress Cataloging-in-Publication Data
Names: Godwin, Jane, 1964– author. | Bell, Davina, author. | Blackwood, Freya, illustrator.
Title: Baby day / Jane Godwin and Davina Bell ; illustrated by Freya Blackwood.
Other titles: Birthday baby
Description: First edition. | New York : Atheneum Books for Young Readers, 2019. | Summary: Illustrations and easy-to-read text
celebrate a baby's first birthday and all of the different babies who attend the party, whether friendly, sleepy, or wriggly.
Identifiers: LCCN 2017008272 | ISBN 9781481470346 (hardcover) | ISBN 9781481470353 (eBook)
Subjects: | CYAC: Babies—Fiction. | Birthdays—Fiction. | Parties—Fiction. | Individuality—Fiction.
Classification: LCC PZ7.G54377 Bab 2018 | DDC [E]—dc23
LC record available at https://lccn.loc.gov/2017008272

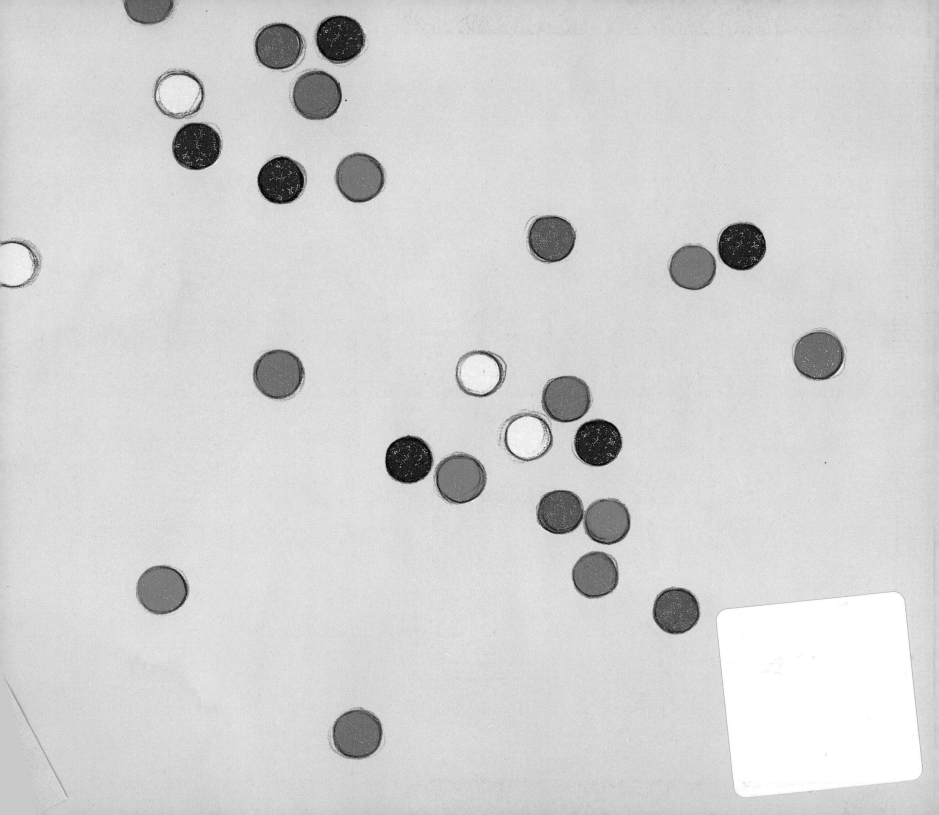